The Legend of Gilgamesh

A legend from Mesopotamia (now Iraq)

Geraldine McCaughrean

Illustrated by
Ian McCaughrean

D1614547

CONTENTS

OXFORD
UNIVERSITY PRESS

Dear Reader,

The epic of Gilgamesh is the oldest recorded story in the world. It was originally carved on twelve clay tablets which, over thousands of years, were smashed into thousands of shards. Even now, scholars cannot be sure of the right order for reading them. Some episodes are still lost.

Gilgamesh was probably a real king. If so he ruled, more than four thousand years ago, over the city of Uruk, in Mesopotamia (now Iraq). He may have led expeditions into neighbouring lands, to fetch back timber for his grand building projects.

Every storyteller tells a story in his or her own way. This is my version. You might tell it altogether differently. Just so long as someone somewhere is telling the legend of Gilgamesh, he and the many other characters in the story will live on, won't they?

Geraldine McCaughrean

Chapter 1
Heaven sent

Gilgamesh dreamed that a meteor crashed to Earth at his feet. Everyone came running to marvel at it.

'So huge!'

'What if it had fallen on my house?'

'What if it had fallen on me?'

They pushed against it, but twelve men together could not budge it.

In his dream, Gilgamesh put a strip of leather round the rock and, resting the strap across his forehead, strained to lift it. The crowd gasped: 'It must weigh more than a hundred sacks of grain!' Gilgamesh, though, lifted the meteor clear of the ground and staggered with it to his mother. But just as he arrived at her door ... he woke.

So he carried her the dream, instead.

His mother, Ninsun, understood the meaning of dreams. 'The gods are sending you a visitor – some foreign king or sage. Someone of great importance.'

'This is not the first time I have dreamed a strange dream,' he confessed.

'Tell me,' said Ninsun.

'I dreamed I was walking through the streets of Uruk, and I saw an axe lying on the ground. I had to pick it up. I had to own it! So I slipped it through my belt and wore it by my side, and I was so pleased to have it, I can't explain ...' He broke off; it sounded so foolish.

But his mother did not laugh. 'Ah! Now I see. It's someone much more important than a king or a sage. The gods are sending you a *friend*!'

Gilgamesh frowned. He had seen rocks before, and axes. But even in a dream, he had never had such a thing as a friend. The idea was as strange to him as a piece of Heaven falling to Earth.

* * *

The people of Uruk certainly did not see their king as a friend. Gilgamesh was wearing them down, wearing them out. So much life, so much energy. He was forever making war. For what? For the excitement of it. Every month he ordered the building of some new tower or palace. For what? For the sake of touching the sky. And who did the building? The people of Uruk, toiling under the lash of the noonday sun.

They prayed to the gods: 'Save us from this king of ours! Marvellous he may be, but he wears us like the soles of his sandals and we are wearing thin!'

The name *Gilgamesh* spread far and wide, beyond the curved walls of Uruk, beyond the river, out into the wild places. The sighs of the people of Uruk set the lakes trembling. Their unhappiness hissed in the long grass.

Chapter 2
The wild man of mud

So Aruru, goddess of beginnings, scooped up
a lump of earth and shaped it into a man. And
that was Enkidu. The clay she used was full of
tree bark, leaf mould and husks. The man she
made turned out shaggy and rough, with a pelt
of matted hair and a bark-brown face. He lived
among the animals, drank milk from the wild
asses, whistled up the birds and stroked the wild
dogs. He knew them as if they were brothers or
sisters – but was he truly ass, or dog, or bird?

When he glimpsed huntsmen or shepherds,
they puzzled him. Though they were small
and weak and hairless, they reminded him
of the reflection he saw when he drank at
the waterhole.

Eavesdropping, he learned their language.
Stealthily watching them round their campfire,
Enkidu heard them talk. The talk was often of
mighty King Gilgamesh.

• *Aruru:* (say) 'ah-roo-roo'.   • *Enkidu:* (say) 'en-kee-doo'.

'A tyrant and a marvel, so they say.'

'A blessing and a curse, I heard.'

'A dream and a nightmare.'

'Not that I've ever seen him myself.'

'Count yourself lucky!'

Listening, Enkidu the wild man flared into a great rage. 'Is this any way for a father of his people to behave? Trampling his own people? I shall go to Uruk and challenge this Gilgamesh! I shall pound him into clay!'

* * *

Meanwhile, King Gilgamesh was thinking of marrying. Every day he shut himself up in the Temple of Ishtar, the goddess of love, and people outside could hear the slap of his sandals on the floor. Rumour had it that the King might even marry the terrible Ishtar herself!

Then along came something to set the marketplace buzzing. The crowds parted in fear. A new face in Uruk! A man almost as alarming as Gilgamesh. The crowd murmured and gasped.

'He is the size of Gilgamesh!'

'Shorter.'

'Yes, but thicker set!'

'A wild man, brought up with lions!'

Gilgamesh came out of the temple and turned towards his mother's house. His mind was made up. He would woo and marry the goddess of love. She was surely the only fitting bride for him ...

Enkidu stepped out into his path. Gilgamesh, lost in thought, made to go round him. Enkidu stuck out a foot and tripped him up. Gilgamesh grabbed Enkidu's arm as he fell and pulled him down, too.

They wrestled in the doorways of the houses, their bulk smashing doors and bringing down the doorposts. They grappled each other head-to-head, chest-to-chest, barging through the walls of buildings.

First Gilgamesh was on his back, his face full of the wild man's hair, then the King was

on top of Enkidu, their hands locked together. Scattering chickens, demolishing goat pens, overturning pails, the two men wrestled for hour after hour. Then Gilgamesh caught Enkidu off-balance, and with a twist of the body, hurled him to the ground.

Enkidu lay winded. Gilgamesh snorted out a triumphant laugh as he struggled to catch his breath. Then Enkidu, who was lying on his back watching the fearful stars blinking down between the high buildings, laughed out loud. 'There's no one in the world like you, Gilgamesh!'

Gilgamesh sat down with his back against a wall. It was an unfamiliar feeling: to be tired out. The two men looked at one another. Enkidu flexed his arms and Gilgamesh flexed his, and they fell on each other again.

But this time they hugged. They hugged each other with the passion of new friends who knew they would stick together through thick and thin, come what may, do or die.

Chapter 3
Do or die

Like the axe in his dream, Gilgamesh wore
Enkidu at his side. They swore never to be
parted. 'I must have been mad to have been
thinking about marriage,' he told Enkidu,
'especially to Ishtar!'

Gilgamesh taught Enkidu the ways of the city
– how to eat at the table, how to drink from a
cup, how to wash and walk upright rather than
dragging his knuckles along the ground. Then
Enkidu taught Gilgamesh the ways of the wild:
how the honey ant gathers its winter food, how
mistletoe grows without a root, how water can
be mined out of the driest desert.

They wrestled and raced and hunted and
talked. The people of Uruk breathed a sigh of
relief and gave thanks to the gods.

Enkidu had roamed far afield and seen things which Gilgamesh had never seen. He had swum in the twin rivers of the world – in both the Tigris and the Euphrates.

He had stood on the mount where the ark ran aground after the Great Flood. He had even seen the monstrous Huwawa, magical guardian of the Cedar Forest.

One day, as Gilgamesh showed Enkidu around the city, he pointed out the carved stone friezes recording the deeds of Uruk's great men.

'Where are the deeds of Gilgamesh?' asked Enkidu.

'Here!' cried Gilgamesh, spread-eagling himself against a blank stretch of wall. 'So far I've done nothing worth carving in stone. But soon! Soon, Enkidu! You and I are going on such an adventure that no wall will be large enough to record it!'

'We are?' Enkidu too flattened himself against the wall. 'Where? When? Now?' The very ends of his long hair crackled with energy.

• *Tigris:* (say) 'ty-gris'. • *Euphrates:* (say) 'you-frey-teez'.
• *Huwawa:* (say) 'hoo-wah-wah'.

'You gave me the idea! Who's the most frightening foe in the whole world?'

Enkidu racked his brains. 'Gilgamesh!'

Gilgamesh laughed. 'Someone far more dangerous! We are going to fight Huwawa and kill him, and bring home cedar wood to build new gates for Uruk.'

Enkidu stepped away from the wall. 'Ah now, listen. You're forgetting, I've seen Huwawa. He's monstrously big! The trees are small alongside him. He never sleeps. When a fox stamps sixty leagues away, Huwawa hears it. He lives for battle! He was made for the sole purpose of guarding the forest. He has some kind of magic … You can't go close without your strength ebbing away. If you'd seen Huwawa …'

'I would have killed him already!' declared Gilgamesh. 'What are you afraid of?'

'Of getting killed,' said Enkidu candidly.

Gilgamesh spread his arms high above his head. 'But if we are killed we will have died gloriously, won't we? And our names will be written in clouds of glory on the noonday sky! Fame is everything, Enkidu, isn't it? Why live if you don't make a mark on the world? Do or die!'

A surge of love and pride rushed through Enkidu. 'Do or die!' he cried, and closed his own hand around the King's upraised fist.

'People of Uruk!' cried Gilgamesh, standing on the sill of his window in the great palace. 'I go to the Cedar Forest, to cut the wood for new city gates. I will have to do battle with the monster Huwawa, who guards the forest. So pray for me, and make offerings daily to the sun! I shall bring back more than cedar; I shall bring back glory!'

The crowd burst into song. Perhaps they were rejoicing in the idea of new gates. Perhaps they were simply looking forward to peace and quiet while Gilgamesh was gone. The King's elderly counsellors were less happy. 'You are young and rash, Gilgamesh. Please think again. This is too dangerous!'

Gilgamesh only laughed. 'What do you want me to do, gentlemen? Sit safe at home till I'm as old as you and do nothing with my life?'

The counsellors shook their wise old heads: there is no telling young people what they don't want to hear. 'Ah well,' they sighed, 'if anyone can do this thing, it is Gilgamesh and Enkidu.'

Ninsun, Gilgamesh's mother sent for Enkidu. 'Oh, look after him, Enkidu! Bring Gilgamesh home safely. I'm relying on you!'

The wild man bowed his head. For the first time, he realised that there was someone else in the world who loved Gilgamesh as much as he did.

* * *

What a way it was to the land of the Cedar Forest! The friends walked fifty leagues a day, and did in three days what it would take others six weeks to do. Even then, they still had to cross seven mountains before they reached the Cedar Forest gate.

Carved on it were the words:

DO NOT ENTER!
CUT NO TREES, ON PAIN
OF DEATH.
THIS FOREST IS PROTECTED
BY HUWAWA, TERROR OF
THE EARTH.

Yet the woodlands beyond the gate looked so peaceful. Birdsong rippled.

Enkidu shoved the gate open. Immediately his knees sagged. His head spun. His hands prickled as though stabbed by a thousand splinters. He staggered backwards. 'Gilgamesh! Don't go in there! The magic is too strong!'

Gilgamesh, though, was already whistling his way along the broad green pathways of the forest.

In the centre of the forest stood a green mountain, its peak hidden in cloud. Its slopes seemed a perfect place to sleep, and the friends stretched out on the ground. Still, they slept back-to-back, so as to wake one another at the first sign of danger.

At midnight, Enkidu was woken by Gilgamesh sitting bolt upright. The King's eyes glistened in the dark. 'I dreamed the top of the mountain melted, and the Earth spewed out fire, rock and so much ash that the sun turned black! What does it mean?'

Enkidu laughed. 'It means we've come to the land of volcanoes, friend,' he said. 'In these parts the mountains erupt like spots on a cheek.'

'But I dreamed the Earth shook, too! Dust flew up so thick I couldn't breathe – couldn't see. Everything around me caught fire! What does it mean?'

Again Enkidu laughed. 'It means we are in the land of earthquakes! The world's surface is like snakeskin – now and then the scales twitch, and

the Earth shakes. What else?'

'I dreamed of a bull,' said Gilgamesh. 'Not just a bull, I mean: a giant of a bull. It was head down and charging right at you, and there was nothing I could do. Nothing! Nothing!'

Enkidu scratched his head. 'Huwawa is nothing like a bull,' he said, puzzled. 'His face is like a lion and he has fangs like a dragon. I don't know why you should dream of a ... Gilgamesh?'

But Gilgamesh had fallen asleep, his head on Enkidu's shoulder. When daylight came, he was still asleep. Enkidu pushed him. Enkidu shook him. Enkidu took hold of him by the ears and banged his head on the ground, but he would not wake up. Huwawa's magic was at work. The whole day came and went, and still Gilgamesh slept.

Enkidu was panic-stricken. 'Wake up!' he bellowed in his friend's ear. 'Wake up! Do you want Huwawa to find you like this?'

He slapped Gilgamesh. He rolled him down the hill. He up-ended a waterskin over his friend

– empty! Enkidu ran and ran, until at last he heard the soft tinkle of trickling water. Splashing into the stream, he scooped the waterskin through the cool, delicious water. Then back he ran and emptied it over the King's face.

At last, the dark brown eyes opened. Stretching himself, Gilgamesh picked up his breast plate and put it on. He was perfectly calm. 'Let us go and meet our enemy.'

Enkidu kicked aside his bow in disgust. 'You go if you like, but I'm going back. You have no idea … You don't know what you are up against! Me, I'll go back and tell your mother how brave you are, how heroic, how glorious … how dead.'

Gilgamesh calmly strung his bow. 'Don't launch the funeral barge yet. What can go wrong with the two of us side by side?'

'Do you really want me to say?' said Enkidu.

Inside his cedar wood house, Huwawa cocked his giant head on one side and listened. His smile curled like the bark from a silver birch. He reached out and took down his first cloak of

splendour. Six more cloaks hung alongside it, woven out of magic. He opened his door, stuck out his head and bellowed.

'WHO HAS COME INTO THE FOREST? LET HIM DIE!'

All the pine cones fell from the trees. As Huwawa looked, the beams from his eyes scythed down trees. He nodded his head, and evil magic rolled through the forest, bluer and deeper than drifts of bluebells. Then he stepped out of doors. The green forest was like grass around his feet. He blotted out the sun.

Gilgamesh, caught in the coal-black shadow, looked up. 'Oh, Enkidu,' he said. He had never thought anything could be so big. 'Oh Shamash, look kindly on me!'

Shamash, the sun god, looked down and saw Gilgamesh and his friend: like two tiny ants in the path of an elephant's stampede.

Shamash breathed in, fetching the warm winds. He reached out to sea and grasped the north wind and the waterspouts, lightning and the electricity of eels. He turned about and about, and the elements were twisted into a single whiplash, its thongs sharp with hail and sleet.

Huwawa ran back into his house and grabbed his second cloak. He had been formed to protect the forest, and even the sun, his own master, could not call him to heel.

Gilgamesh was wielding his axe now, hacking at the wall of the lodge. But there were seven walls, one inside another, and inside the seventh, Huwawa, bellowing flame and destruction.

Huwawa put on the third of his seven cloaks.

Thanks to Shamash, the shining sun god, more and more winds of Heaven were piling up around the monster's lodge. They turned back Huwawa's powers like a mirror turns back light. Huwawa put on the fourth of his seven cloaks; the walls of his house bowed outwards, so great was the magic within. Huwawa put on the fifth and sixth of his seven cloaks and, for twenty thousand leagues, the Cedar Forest trembled.

At last the seventh cedar wall fell, and Gilgamesh and Enkidu, axes in hand, came face to face with Huwawa. Seven cloaks billowed round him like a rainbow; magic shone from his open mouth, from the heels of his hands, from the fabric of his skin.

Huwawa was magnificent.

He was also a prisoner, lassoed in chains of the sun god's making. Twisted cords of wind and heat bound him. 'Let me go, Gilgamesh!' he said. 'Spare me and I shall cut down the trees myself, to build you your city gates!'

Gilgamesh hesitated. He glanced sideways at Enkidu.

'Don't listen to him!' urged Enkidu. 'It's a trick. Kill him!'

Gilgamesh swung back his axe over one shoulder. 'But Enkidu … if we kill him, all that glory will be lost to the world for ever!'

'Don't let him fool you, Gilgamesh!' (Enkidu was not sure how long those ropes of wind would hold Huwawa.)

It took three blows to kill Huwawa, guardian of the Cedar Forest. When he fell, he flattened the trees for acres around. His scorching glory snuffed out, he became no more than a mound of vegetable matter, a hummock in the landscape. Dead.

Gilgamesh, walking the length of the dead body, was exultant. He had survived! He was alive – even more alive than before. All the colours of the forest were brighter, the birdsong sweeter, the smells more delicious. It made him dizzy with joy to think that he and his dearest

friend were still alive. They found the tallest cedar tree in the entire forest and felled it with a deafening hiss of leaves. From this the carpenters of Uruk would make new city gates.

Gilgamesh washed in the river, put on clean robes and made an offering of cold water to the sun god Shamash. When he held up the silver bowl, the noonday heat drank it up in steamy white sips.

Looking down, Ishtar, goddess of love, saw him – a young man, triumphant, face shining with happiness: King Gilgamesh. As much as Gilgamesh had wanted that cedar tree, now Ishtar wanted to marry him.

Chapter 4
Marry me

'Gilgamesh! Gilgamesh! My hero!'

Gilgamesh spun round. Through the perfumed smoke of the temple came a woman astounding in every way. Her hair spilled down, like water over-brimming a beaker, from the crown of her head to the soles of her feet. It was Ishtar, goddess of love. 'I watched you fight that monster Huwawa! My heart was in my mouth ...' She brought her face close up against his. Her breath smelled of nutmeg and roses. 'I love you, King of Uruk. Marry me.'

Gilgamesh breathed her in. Her perfume made him dizzy.

'I'll give you fame and victory! A chariot with golden wheels and storm demons to pull it. Your enemies will lie like carpet under your feet ...!'

Gilgamesh put a finger to her lips. 'And I'll give you sacrifices, goddess. That is my duty. I always have and I always will. But as for marrying you … Oh no! Not for all the honey in the hive.'

Ishtar's jaw dropped.

'I'm flattered, but frankly I'd rather juggle scorpions. I've heard the stories. Being loved by you is like being struck by a falling building.' He counted off on his fingers all the young men Ishtar had loved. 'Remember that shepherd? The one who played his flute for you? He thought he was the happiest man alive – till you got bored and turned him into a wolf. Where is he these days? Still howling at the moon?

'That horse who took your fancy: what did you give him? Spurs and a whip and nothing but muddy water to drink in the end.

'That bird who sang for you – the one with rainbow plumes? You smashed him like a tennis ball. Now he sits on a branch and weeps, "My wing! My poor broken wing!"'

Ishtar opened and shut her mouth, but no words came out.

'The trouble with you, madam, you start by kissing and end by cursing. I would rather wear tight shoes for the rest of my life than be married to you!'

With a laugh, Gilgamesh dodged her clawing fingernails, skipped out into the clean, white sunlight and ran to find Enkidu.

Ishtar ran all the way to Heaven and threw herself down at her father's feet, weeping bitterly. 'Kill Gilgamesh!' she sobbed. 'Destroy him! He has insulted me!'

Anu fingered his beard. 'How? What did he say?'

'He listed all my lovers and what I had done to them!'

Anu said, 'And? Was it untrue?'

'He called me a ... a ...'

Anu leaned forwards expectantly. 'Yes? What did he call you?'

'A falling building! A pair of tight shoes! Don't laugh! Never mind *what* he called me! He must be put down! Loose the Bull of Heaven and destroy him!'

Anu was shocked. 'Do you know what you are asking, Ishtar? If I loose the Bull of Heaven, it will be seven years before Uruk recovers. Famine and drought! Destruction! Have you thought of the innocent people who will die?'

Ishtar flapped a hand. 'Yes, yes. But Gilgamesh

must pay. *Well?*' Her tears splashed like hot lead on the pavements of Heaven.

Anu looked at his daughter. Anger made her ugly; it makes all faces ugly. Her teeth were bared and her eyes were bloodshot with shouting. It was plain there would be no peace until Ishtar got her way.

'Not the Bull of Heaven, daughter. Choose some lesser punishment.'

'If you don't give me what I want,' hissed Ishtar, her voice so menacing that even Anu shivered, 'I shall smash the bolts on the gates of the Underworld. I shall loose all the souls of the dead ...'

'*Ishtar!*'

'Up they will come out of the ground, hungry for food. Wait until the dead begin to EAT!' Anu shuddered in disgust. 'Stop, Ishtar ...'

'... the dead loosed from the Underworld to eat the living!'

'*Ishtar, enough!*'

'*Well?*'

'I shall loose the Bull of Heaven, daughter ... But I am very sorry to see a man punished simply for speaking the truth.'

* * *

In the city of Uruk, red dust trickled from the sandstone buildings and all the dogs began to bark. Cockerels crowed in the middle of the night, and dates fell from the palm trees in fat, black splats. The Bull of Heaven was coming ...

Then everyone in Uruk was awake and running – yelling and pointing out over the plain. The goddess Ishtar was coming out of the dawn, leading the Bull of Heaven, and no one had seen such a sight in the history of the world. Here was Destruction wearing hide and hooves and horns.

From the city wall, Gilgamesh and Enkidu watched. The bull was as big as a herd of elephants. Its horns, jewel-plated in precious lapis lazuli, were as huge as the prow and stern of a ship. Ishtar led it to the far bank of the river.

'How women do hate to be spurned,' said Enkidu softly. He could smell the sweat in his friend's palms – smell his own fear, come to that.

Then the beast stamped, and there was no more thinking. The Earth simply opened up. Acres of soil fell away into a bottomless hole, and with it fell a hundred young men.

Again the bull stamped the ground, head down, the hump of its back quaking. Within the city, the grain stores broke open like eggs, spilling their contents. Carved friezes cracked and fell in shards. Towers swayed and crumbled into dust, and a jagged pit yawned in the ground, swallowing up two hundred warriors of Uruk. The river Euphrates cascaded down into darkness. A single scream of terror hung in the air.

At the third stamp, the very walls of Uruk wavered like sheets of water. Enkidu was jarred off his feet and struck his head against the parapet. Pain paralysed him: it seemed to sing through his skull and unstring his spine. Then he was on his feet again: 'Quick! Before it can charge the city gate!'

Launching himself off the high wall, Enkidu landed between the very horns of the bull, grasping them like the shafts of a cart. The foam from its nostrils burst into his face, blinding him.

Gilgamesh leapt down as well, sword drawn.

'Well, friend? Didn't we say we would make a name for ourselves?' called Enkidu. 'Strike behind the horns if you can!'

Bucking stiff-legged, turning and turning on the spot, the Bull of Heaven lashed Enkidu with its thick, hairy cable of a tail and sent him sprawling along its back. But Gilgamesh was there to vault over the nose and take hold of the horns in Enkidu's place, to wrench them round until the beast was brought to a standstill.

Meanwhile, Enkidu slithered over the bull's rump, grabbing the tail as he went, pulling it like a bell rope, hanging on even when the dust from under its iron hooves enveloped him in gritty darkness. Digging in with his heels, he hauled on the tail – quick, wrenching tugs which took the bull's attention away from the flimsy gate, away from Gilgamesh straddling its neck.

There was a flash of light, a hiss and a thud. The blade of Gilgamesh's sword cut the bull's neck – between nape and horns.

For long seconds, the bull held still, the foam dripping from its nostrils into a sudsy pool between its feet. Then it staggered sideways, crashed against the walls of Uruk and lurched the other way. It stumbled as far as the river before falling into what little water was left, turning it blood red.

Enkidu sat on the ground, holding his head. Up on the wall – a wall now covered with jagged cracks – Ishtar the goddess of love, let out a howl of pure hatred. Red dust had painted her the colour of rage. Tears burst through her tightly shut lids, making runnels in the dust. 'You have butchered the lovely Bull of Heaven! Weep, Uruk, at what they have done!'

The women of Uruk did not need telling.

They wept, not for the carcass lying in the river mud, but for three hundred young men swallowed up by the earth, for the empty river, for the ruin of the city.

Gilgamesh, not heeding the women, stood on the body of the great bull. 'See the horns, plated in lapis? I shall fill them with oil and offer the oil to the gods! Then I shall hang them on the wall of my palace to remind me how I slew the Bull of Heaven!'

The remaining men of Uruk, happy to be alive, cheered and carried Gilgamesh and Enkidu shoulder-high into the battered city.

'*Who fought the Bull of Heaven?*' shouted the little boys and the little girls shouted back, '*Gilgamesh! Gilgamesh!*'

Only the mothers and old women stood in their doorways, shawls drawn tight under their chins, silent.

Ishtar, goddess of love, chewed on her plait of hair and cursed Gilgamesh under her breath. 'Death to Gilgamesh and Enkidu. A curse on their friendship and on their happiness!'

* * *

Enkidu's head ached where it had slammed against the wall. Throughout the celebrations, he felt a little sick. That night he slept deeply, despite drums banging in his skull. He dreamed, too.

The gods were talking. Shamash was speaking: 'It was Gilgamesh who killed Huwawa.'

'But it was Enkidu who cut down the tallest tree.'

Enkidu tried to speak, tried to put across his side of the argument. But as in all dreams, his hands would not lift and his shouts only came out as whimpers.

Shamash was saying, 'They asked for my help and permission. They made an offering to me afterwards.'

The King of the gods, Enlil, interrupted. 'But now the Bull of Heaven has been killed: law demands that someone must pay. It is simply a matter of deciding who, Gilgamesh or Enkidu, Gilgamesh or Enkidu, Gilgamesh or Enkidu, Gilgamesh or ...'

Enkidu woke with the name of his friend on his lips: 'Gilgamesh or ...' He was wet with sweat and shivering. He had to go and tell Gilgamesh – to warn him. Dreams were not just leaves blown down from the day before. Dreams were omens. Dreams were messages. He slipped his legs off the bed and tried to stand up.

But the roaring inside his head was like the Bull of Heaven bellowing. He covered his eyes, but the light still seared through to his brain. Sweat crawled down his body like a swarm of beetles, and his guts ached.

'Gilgamesh!' he tried to call, but his own name emerged instead. 'Enkidu! Enkidu must die!'

Chapter 5

Death

Gilgamesh sponged his friend's face and put a cup of water to his lips. 'Soon be well, 'kidu. Soon.'

Enkidu turned his face away. The pain inside his head was like an axe-blow. 'The gods say I must die.'

Gilgamesh snorted. 'Everyone dreams bad dreams when they're sick. Come on, man! Heroes like us have nothing to be afraid of!'

Two days later, Enkidu was powerless to sit up, unable to eat. A fear sprang up in Gilgamesh, despite himself. 'Soon be well, friend,' he kept saying, but Enkidu only groaned. 'I'll go to the temple. I'll go and pray for you. The gods will listen to me.

'Shamash listened before. I'll have the goldsmiths make a statue of you. Yes, that's what! I'll tell them to make a golden statue of you and I'll offer it up to the gods. Why don't I do that?

Yes. Wait here. Don't worry. Everything will be all right!' Then he was gone, running towards the temple, shouting commands, summoning his craftsmen.

Enkidu was left alone on his bed. The sun moved round, and a ray of sunlight struck him in the face like a fist.

'Oh Shamash, hear my curses!' he told the sun. 'A curse on this city that brought me out of the wild places. A curse on the day I came to Uruk. A curse on the day I ever ...' He broke off, panting for breath; his skull seemed to be squeezing the blood from his brain.

The window-hanging blew out in a draught and set the sunlight dancing. It was as if a voice came rustling in at the window along with that breeze – a voice so soft that he strained to hear it.

'Enkidu. Oh, Enkidu. Why curse the past? Would you rather you had never gone questing after Huwawa, never fought the Bull of Heaven, never written your name into history? The city you curse is holding its breath now, praying for Enkidu. Gilgamesh is kneeling in the temple, weeping salt tears. Don't you see? Now Gilgamesh will be the wild man. He will mourn you like a wolf baying at the moon and wander the world looking for comfort ... Would you really choose to have lived without such a friend?'

Enkidu's fist closed around the empty air containing the sunbeam. 'I call them back! Every last curse! *Be my witness, Shamash, I call them back!* Never have met Gilgamesh? That would have been never to have lived at all. We came alive together, he and I. We made sense of it all. We made sense ...'

He let his hand fall. Fever made the room throb and crinkle like the walls of a bread oven, and his tears were scalding hot. Yet he was easier in his mind.

Gilgamesh came bounding back from the temple, hopeful, full of optimism. Now Enkidu would get better.

It took only one glance to know he was mistaken.

His friend's eyes were shut. Gilgamesh sank his fingers in to Enkidu's hair and shook him.

'Wake up! I thought you were ...'

Then Gilgamesh cradled his friend in his arms and his tears soaked the crumpled pillow.

For seven days Gilgamesh struggled like a man in mid-ocean, trying to keep a friend afloat. Below, in the depths, lurked Death. First it would swallow Enkidu; next Gilgamesh. Life was nothing but treading water until the sharks came along ...

'It's shameful for a man to die like this!' said Enkidu. 'Ishtar hasn't just killed me; she has shamed me, too ... I can't see! I can't hear! Why is everywhere so quiet?'

Gilgamesh eased his arm from under Enkidu and stood up, stiffly. He went to the window with its broad sill and stepped outside. His voice carried loud over the early morning city. 'Quiet? It's not quiet, friend! Can't you hear the people of Uruk weeping for Enkidu? Can't you hear them? Listen! And the friends you made – so many friends.' He raised his voice still higher. 'You! You animals in the wilderness! You knew him in his wild days, and you're weeping for him, aren't you?

'You trees in the Cedar Forest – you're weeping for him, aren't you? Every place we ever went, every blade of grass we trod underfoot, every river we ever drank from – all the mountains and all the valleys – they're weeping for you!

'Everyone is mourning Enkidu. Listen! Can't you hear? *Why* can't you hear?'

He went back to the man on the bed, still lamenting. But Enkidu's eyes stayed shut. Gilgamesh laid a hand on the wild man's heart, but knew he would feel no beat. 'And me, 'kidu. And me. I'm weeping. Wake up now. Wake up and see how the world prizes you. Don't sleep your life away. Wake up now. Don't get lost in the dark.'

Gilgamesh covered his friend with a sheet of silk, carefully, carefully, carefully.

Then he let loose the madness chained up inside him. He smashed everything precious,

everything beautiful, ripping down hangings,
hurling ornaments out of the window. He tore
his clothes into shreds.

Then, when the rage was past, he sat down again by his friend, panting, one hand on the silk. 'Wake up now. Please wake up.'

The whole household gathered outside the door, anxious, whispering, calling out, offering to carry the body away for burial.

But Gilgamesh would not let them in. He fixed his eyes on his friend's shrouded face, and he willed the silk to stir. All that day he sat with the body. All of the next day, too. 'Wake up now. Please wake up.'

For seven days and seven nights his tears made splashy patterns on the tiles at his feet. Then, on the eighth day he stopped crying. The truth fell on him, like a ton of sand: no amount of crying was going to bring Enkidu back. His death went on forever.

He got up and went outside. The little golden statue of Enkidu – his bribe to the gods – stood on a table outside the Temple of Shamash. Beside it Gilgamesh set one bowl filled with honey and another filled with butter: offerings to the gods.

Flies drowned themselves in the honey, and the butter melted from pale gold into oil. Gilgamesh would not curse the gods for taking his friend away from him. After all, they were not really to blame. It was unbearable, and yet he had to bear it.

Just so long as they did not expect him to die too.

Chapter 6
Afraid of nothing

Gilgamesh was never going to die. He had made up his mind. Having seen death at close quarters, he knew that it was not for him. It made a nonsense of bravery, it made fame worthless. No, he would arrange Enkidu's funeral, then leave Uruk – it held nothing for him now – and go in search of the secret.

'What secret? What is it you want to know?' his mother asked, alarmed by the madness in her son's eyes.

'The secret of immortality, of course,' said Gilgamesh. 'What I have to do, where I have to go to live forever.'

'Oh, but Gilgamesh! Son! No one lives forever! Death comes to us all in the end. It is just a matter of how ...'

'That's not true!'

Ninsun was alarmed. His voice was so harsh. He grabbed her by the wrist and led her through the palace yards and gardens to where a frieze decorated one of the great walls.

As a child, Gilgamesh had sat and gazed at it for hours. It was his favourite story: of the Flood and the man who saved the world from ending. There was a boat riding on the floodwaters, and on top of it stood a man, hands upraised.

'*He* didn't die!' Gilgamesh jabbed a finger at the carving. 'Utnapishtim was made immortal by the gods. If they can grant immortality to him, they can grant it to me! All I have to do is find Utnapishtim and ask him the secret!'

Ninsun trembled for her son. The death of his friend had driven him mad. He was not eating, not washing, not sleeping. Already his handsome face had aged ten years. She put out a hand to touch his cheek, but he broke away from her and was gone, like a horse bolting. 'Gilgamesh! Son! Come back! Where are you going? *Come back!*'

The King of Uruk ran out of his city into the wild places. Soon his curled and glossy hair hung in a matted mass down his back, and his kingly robes were ragged. He drank at the same muddy waterholes as gazelles and hogs.

He asked the beasts and the bushes and the trees, 'Where can I find Utnapishtim?' but they did not answer.

The trees put their heads together and whispered. Gilgamesh despised them: trees lived and died without a struggle. He envied them: each spring they came back to life. Not Enkidu. He would never come back.

He did not stop to eat. Once he reached the stony wilderness, there was no food anyway, and he was always thirsty. The fat melted off him like butter, leaving his limbs thin, his wrists and ankle-bones looking too big. In the daytime the sun burned him raw, and sweat trickled down his hair.

By night, the cold was so terrible that blood from a cut froze before it touched the ground. But on he went, as if Death was dogging his trail. At last he came to the Mountains of Mashu. They were so high that they pierced the sky itself, so jagged that they sawed land from sky. 'O moon god, Sin!' Gilgamesh prayed aloud. 'Guard my sleeping hours and bring me safely through this night.'

Gilgamesh walked into the foothills until daylight failed completely, then he climbed into a tree and slept. When he woke, his eyelids were gummy with dust. He rolled over and only narrowly saved himself from falling out of the tree. Beneath him, prancing, wrestling or rolling on their backs in the dew, were thirty or forty lions, lionesses and cubs. Their golden bodies were lithe as river water. They glowed with health and energy and life.

Gilgamesh hated them for being so alive.

He leapt out of the tree, sword drawn, caught them by their tails and smashed them one against another. He jumped and stamped on them, wrestled and throttled them. Afterwards he ate lion steak and replaced his city clothes with a lion's pelt knotted by the paws around his neck. Now the big, lifeless paws patted against his skin as he walked. It soothed him that the lively lions were dead.

Beyond the foothills, the Mountains of Mashu rose up, sheer and smooth as glass. On this side lay the Lands of Men, on the far side the Garden of the Gods. There was a gate, a way through. He knew that much. The sun itself, in sinking each night, used the gate to pass through the mountain.

But Gilgamesh had not reckoned upon the monsters who stood guard over the gate: Scorpionman and Scorpionwoman.

They balanced on crackling, scuttling legs, heads helmeted with black scales, and both had beards as black as thunderclouds.

Arching over each head, hung the poisonous tip of a scorpion's tail. No arrow, fire or sandstorm could harm them – not even the heat of the sun as it rolled past each evening.

They rarely had to use their stings: the very sight of them drained a man's heart of blood

and left him dead of shock. When they saw
Gilgamesh striding towards them, they were
astonished.

'He must be one of the immortals,' said
Scorpionman.

'Well, some of him is human at least,' said
Scorpionwoman. 'Can't you smell the flesh and
blood?' She called, '*Halt! Who dares approach?*'

'I am looking for Utnapishtim the faraway,
who lives beyond the Garden of the Gods. My
name is Gilgamesh, King of Uruk. Open the gate
and let me through. There are things I have to
ask Utnapishtim – things only he can tell me.'

The Scorpionguards trembled: a sound like a
million jostling crabs.

'To do that, you would need to travel through
the mountain – twelve leagues without light!
What is so important that you'd attempt the
impossible? Aren't you afraid, Gilgamesh?
Do you know nothing of fear? We admire your
courage. We do! But turn back now, if you
love life!'

The expression on Gilgamesh's face made even the Scorpionguards blench. His soul looked out at them through his eyes. That soul was in torment.

'I had a friend,' he told them, 'the best friend a man ever had. His name was Enkidu. We did everything together. But my friend died. He *died*, you hear? I thought that if I bribed the gods, I could save him. I thought if I held him in my arms, the gods couldn't take him away. I thought if I cried long enough, my tears would bring him back to life.

'But I was wrong! Enkidu is dead and gone ... *Not afraid*, did you say? I'm too afraid of Death to care what monsters cross my path: I can't sink any lower into fear. And what good is a king ... what good is a hero *eaten up with terror*?'

The Scorpionguards laid aside their weapons. They heaved open the fire-scorched gate (which they had only ever opened for the sun).

'Pass through before nightfall, Gilgamesh of Uruk. If you do not lose your wits in the dark,

you may reach the other end and stand in the
Garden of the Gods. May the gods grant you an
answer to your questions or an easy death.'

Gilgamesh entered the tunnel. For a while,
when he looked back, Gilgamesh could see their
heads silhouetted against the tunnel's entry, dark
against the daylight, watching him go. But then
the entrance was out of sight and he was plunged
into darkness.

Dark. It was not the dark of night, pricked
through with stars. It was not the darkness of
indoors, with candles or embers in the grate. It was
not the darkness of sleep which is lit by dreams, at
least. No, this was solid dark. The air was as black
as the rock walls to either side. There was no way
of knowing whether the passage bent or its floor
swarmed with cockroaches.

On and on Gilgamesh went, his fingers
touching the wall to either side, his face pushing
forwards, his eyeballs dry with staring helplessly
after light. The darkness had struck him blind and
he had to feel his way, step by step.

When he looked back after one league: dark. When he looked forwards: dark. Inside and outside of his eyelids: dark. Filling his brain: dark.

After two leagues there was no movement of air. Dark to front and back. Dark.

After four and after five leagues, the darkness seemed to seep through his skin. He could taste, smell, see and hear only darkness. The mountain was digesting him.

After six leagues, after seven, there was still no relief. He knew what it was to be buried alive. It was almost like being dead.

After eight, after nine leagues he might as well have been born without eyes. If he had not been mad already with grief, then this darkness would have driven him mad.

After ten leagues a breeze flowed into his face like black water. After eleven, he thought his mind must be playing tricks on him, for a pinprick of light seemed to be dancing, far away, small as an ant's egg.

As he felt his way forward, the pinprick grew to a circle, and through the circle strayed a few weak rays of light.

Blinking and stumbling, blinkering his eyes with both hands, he ran out of the tunnel into … a garden.

It was a garden like no other, for instead of fruit or blossoms on the trees, jewels and precious stones weighed down the golden branches. Jet pips encased in ruby berries, leaves of lapis lazuli, pearls as big as snowberries, branches of coral on trees of onyx, all tinkled and twinkled amid flower heads of silver. Even the dewdrops were diamonds.

After the dark, the absurd magnificence dazzled Gilgamesh. He would have smiled, but the muscles of his face had wasted and stiffened.

'Well,' he thought, 'I've come this far. If I can do that, I can do more.' Enkidu's words came back to him: 'Do or die!'

No truer words.

Do or die.

Chapter 7
Give up

Beyond the garden was the even greater brightness of the sea. Gilgamesh stood and stared out across the water. The sea? He had heard of it but never seen it. Its hugeness made him feel so small.

There was a sea-front bar, its terrace overhung with vines. There was a grape press, too. Whoever lived here clearly grew the grapes and made juice, selling it to passers-by. What passers-by? A woman, as big as a barrel, sat skimming the scum off a vat of grape juice. A veil hid all of her head and body but for her big, bare feet.

Gilgamesh could not see her face through the veil, but she could see him. As he came into view, she straightened a little, then throwing down her skimmer and hoisting up her skirts, she ran for the house. He put on a sprint, but she was already inside and slamming the door. He put out one foot and wedged it in the closing gap.

Siduri leaned all her weight against the door.
Gilgamesh yelped and withdrew his foot: the
woman managed to pin the door shut with her
great bulk. '*Go away, whoever you are!*'

Gilgamesh put his mouth close to the door
and bellowed, 'Let me in or I'll smash in your
walls and kick your grape press into the sea! I am
Gilgamesh, King of Uruk, slayer of Huwawa and
the Bull of Heaven!'

'No, you're not!'

'Yes, I am!'

'Not!'

'Am!'

'Not!'

'I've heard of Gilgamesh,' she panted back
through the door. 'He's young and handsome
and all the women of Uruk swoon after him with
his big dark eyes and his curly hair! And you
come along telling me you're Gilgamesh, you ...
you ... you old *candle wick!*'

Gilgamesh was taken aback. He stepped away
from the door, and Siduri spilled out of doors

at his feet. 'Look at you!' she said. 'You look one hundred and four! You look as if you've walked half the world and seen all its troubles, and slept out in all weathers without a hat! All skin and bone and worry, that's you,' she said accusingly. 'Call yourself Gilgamesh of Uruk?'

'I am!'

'Not!'

'Am!'

'Not!'

'Am!'

'Look at yourself!' she told him.

So Gilgamesh did look into a bowl of grape juice, and even he doubted that the reflection looking back at him was Gilgamesh of Uruk. His cheeks were hollow, his eyes sunken into their sockets, his lips blistered by heat and chapped by cold. His beard was matted with filth, and his hair had turned snow white.

He slapped the reflection into fragments. 'Why shouldn't I be changed?' he said. 'I have travelled half the world, and I have had troubles.

You wouldn't understand – how could a woman understand? I had a friend. The best friend a man could have. His name was Enkidu, and I loved him. Now he's dead. I've just walked through twelve leagues of darkness, and unless I can find Utnapishtim the faraway – I shall die just like Enkidu. Isn't that enough to change a man?'

During the wild and furious lament, Siduri had got to her feet and tidied the mess he had made. 'Sit down and have a drink,' she said cosily while polishing a cup with her veil. 'A few raisins, look. Some good fresh bread: I baked it this morning.' She hummed tunelessly and threw a rock at a seagull stealing sardines from the drying rack. Gradually Gilgamesh grew calmer and dried his tears with one paw of his lion skin.

'Tell me how I can find Utnapishtim, woman,' he said.

'Get washed first, and have a bite to eat ... It can't be had, you know.'

'What can't?'

'This immortality thing.' She filled a beaker with seawater to throw at the skinny cats prowling round the sardine rack.

'When the gods made us, they never meant us to last. No more than a loaf of bread or a chicken's egg. We were meant to grow up, grow old and fall off the twig. You know what you ought to do?'

'Find Utnapishtim, not sit here wasting time', replied Gilgamesh.

'Give up, my dear! Eat, drink and be merry – did you never hear that?

'Oooh, I can recommend it! Honeycakes for breakfast, freshly grilled sardines for lunch. Melon! Now what did the gods ever invent that was better than a melon, eh? Except two melons. A lobster – oooh. Eating cherries in bed, spitting the pips out of the window.

'You're a long time dead – there's another true thing. Grab the day and run with it. What you ought to do is *get married*. Children. That's the shape of happiness. A little hand inside yours.

Someone riding up on your shoulders, laughing out loud. Friends, yes. But a good wife, also! Someone to sit with in the shade. Someone who puts up with you even when you're sour as a lemon. Someone who thinks all your jokes are funny. Someone to come home to after a hard day's ... whatever it is a king does. Someone who thinks you're a hero for killing a cockroach. Live happy! I mean, what good would it do you to live a million years unhappy?'

The cats came coiling and moiling back to their favourite spot.

'Keep your advice for your customers. Just tell me where I can find Utnapishtim.'

Siduri sucked in air through her teeth, so that her veil puckered against her mouth. 'He lives over the water – the other side of the River of Death. And no one crosses over there but Urshanabi the ferryman. He fetches and carries things over to Paradise Shore. You could always ask him ... but he won't take you. It's against his terms of employment, see? Be better off giving up and going home. Seems to me, it's the quality of life that matters, not how long it drags on … *Shoo!*'

Siduri lunged at the cats, flapping her skirts, sending them yowling and hissing down to the beach.

When she turned, Gilgamesh had gone. Siduri chose herself the fattest sardine, poured herself a cup of juice, rested her feet in the water bucket, and ate lunch, flinging the fish heads to the cats and the seagulls. They had known she would; she did it every day.

* * *

Ocean. The edge of all geography, the margin of the known world. What monsters lurked out there, under that glass roof of moving water? Gilgamesh had no idea. The great wisdom of King Gilgamesh came to an end in the surf, and he did not like feeling stupid.

Suddenly he saw it, bobbing on turquoise shallows: the ferry boat. The ferryman was putting a fresh coat of paint on its prow.

Gilgamesh had never captured a boat before. He set about it the same way he would have captured a city. He ran down out of the trees, hollering and yelling and dragging a chunk of wood through the noisy pebbles. He hurtled up to his knees in the water and began smashing at the boat's stern.

Over and over again he hacked at the pegs and pulley and the carved magic symbols. Out of the corner of his eye, he could see the ferryman gaping at him.

Missing his footing, Gilgamesh sat down with a splash. The ferryman threw his paintbrush in the air. 'Now what did you want to go and do that for?'

'*Take me over to Paradise Shore!*' Gilgamesh demanded. '*Take me to see Utnapishtim the faraway!*'

Urshanabi covered his eyes. 'Well, you've made good and sure I can't, haven't you? You just smashed the steering gear.'

Gilgamesh pulled himself to his feet. He said

that being a king gave him the right to smash whatever he liked. 'I am Gilgamesh of Uruk, slayer of Huwawa and the Bull of Heaven!'

'Then you must have fallen on hard times,' said the ferryman. 'I heard you were young and fit. What happened to you?'

So Gilgamesh told him: 'I had a friend. I saw him die. I looked Death in the face, and I was terrified. Terrified. I can't die like that. I don't have to! Utnapishtim didn't! I have to meet him, so he can tell me the secret of immortality.'

Little by little, the slopping sea washed all the bluster out of Gilgamesh. He was left explaining himself, apologising. 'Don't be angry with me, Ferryman. You go there every day. All I'm asking is that you take me there once.'

Urshanabi shook his big, sunburned head. 'You ask more than you know ... But since the steering gear is smashed, I'll need you to cut twelve good long poles of wood from the tallest trees you can find. Then whittle them so that they slot together, end to end. Can you do that? Can kings work with their hands? The crossing takes us over the River of Death. If you or I dip one finger in that river – or splash ourselves – we'll find out all too quickly what death tastes like.'

Humbled, Gilgamesh did as he was told,

though he could not see quite how the twelve poles of wood would help.

He found out soon enough. Putting out to sea, sailing towards the horizon, thinking every moment to tumble over the edge of the world, Gilgamesh had to punt. For a while, one pole was long enough to touch the bottom, but soon two screwed together end to end were not long enough. He screwed on a third and a fourth. Far below, the tip of the massive pole skidded over – what? The hulls of sunken ships? Sleeping turtles? The skulls of drowned men? The scales of sea monsters? Soon six rods were not long enough to touch the bottom.

Some time during the night they entered a different lane – a band of faster moving water. 'Don't let your hands touch the water!' warned Urshanabi, and Gilgamesh knew that they were crossing the River of Death. Not seven nor eight rods, not nine nor ten were enough to touch the bottom of this deepest trench. Gilgamesh screwed on the eleventh and then the very last.

But Urshanabi had got his sums wrong!

'It's not enough!' Gilgamesh told the ferryman. The fast current was starting to carry the boat off course. He dared not push his hands and wrists into the waves to make the massive punt pole touch the bottom.

Then he thought of the mast and began to hack it down.

'But without a sail how shall we break free of the current?' Urshanabi protested.

'*I* shall be the mast!' said Gilgamesh.

Using the mast for a thirteenth rod, their punt pole was just long enough to touch the bottom, and Gilgamesh was able to punt on across the River of Death. Then Urshanabi took the punt pole, and Gilgamesh put on Urshanabi's shirt. His body was so thin that it flapped round him. He stood, arms stretched out to either side, and the west wind filled the shirt like a sail. He thought he would be blown into the sky among the wheeling seagulls. But the boat sailed on.

'It can't be done, you know,' Urshanabi called over his shoulder, casual, matter-of-fact. 'The gods never meant people to live forever. Not your friend, not you, not me. You can ask Utnapishtim, but he'll tell you the same.

'You should stop fretting about death and settle for a good life – do things you can look back on with pride. Make your mark on the world, yes! But then pass the baton to the next runner. That's the way of the world. Run with the baton, then pass it on!'

The boat slowed. Urshanabi turned and saw that Gilgamesh was no longer holding his arms at full stretch, but had his fingers in his ears, so as not to hear the ferryman's talk of giving up.

Chapter 8
Faraway and long ago

What would he be like, Utnapishtim, whom the gods had rewarded with eternal life? Would he look like Enkidu – thickset and shaggy? Would he stand larger than life, radiating life like the zest from a lemon? What towers would he have built on Paradise Shore?

As Gilgamesh stood, arms outstretched, catching the wind in Urshanabi's shirt, he saw the shore coming closer. On it a lion lay sleeping while a fawn calmly cropped grass within the circle of its paws; a wolf was playing alongside a lamb. The air was full of the sound of wood pigeons crooning, and doves sat in heart-shaped pairs on leafy trees.

'No snow ever falls here,' said Urshanabi the ferryman. 'The animals live in perfect peace. No ravens, because there's nothing dead to eat.'

On Paradise Shore only the hours and the years died, moulting like feathers from a swan's back.

A middle-aged couple were sitting together under a halub tree, he in a hammock cracking nuts, she busy brushing a little white goat. At the approach of the boat, the man in the hammock shielded his eyes to look. He had big, sticking-out ears, a thin neck and buck teeth.

'There he is,' said the ferryman, 'but he won't tell you anything different from what I've said.'

Gilgamesh could hardly believe his ears. '*This* is Utnapishtim the immortal? The faraway?' Leaping ashore, he went and stood openly staring at the old man in the hammock.

The man in the hammock did not stir. He simply asked, 'Who are you?'

'I am Gilgamesh, King of Uruk!' he declared, jutting his chin.

'My word,' said the man. 'Kingship must weigh heavy these days. Why so haggard and ragged? You look as if you've seen all the sufferings of the world.'

'Because I have!' said Gilgamesh. 'I've crossed the desert, been scorched by the sun and flayed by frost; travelled through twelve leagues of utter darkness; punted my way across the River of Death. And I have grieved, too. My friend Enkidu died and I've sworn never to die! That's why I've come – to learn the secret of immortality, from the one man who has it ... I thought you would be more ... more ...'

'More what?' Utnapishtim smiled. 'More full of life? Raging and racketing about? Wrestling wild beasts? Slaying giants?'

'Yes! Yes, yes!' Gilgamesh sat down on the ground, weariness suddenly overwhelming him. Utnapishtim's wife, Saba, brought him a drink of pineapple juice.

'Why? What do I have to prove?' said Utnapishtim. 'When a man has only a few years of life, he feels he must pack them full. Say you were given a small trunk and told, "You can carry away with you only as much as you can fit in here." You would cram it full, wouldn't you? Me, I have all the time in the world. Time is not standing at my back with his whip making me dance, making me run, making me strive. I've had time to learn, as well, and I've learned that the important things are few. A companion, contentment, memories, peace.'

He allowed long silences to fall between sentences. 'You should not have troubled coming all this way, Gilgamesh. It is your fate to live and then to die – just as it was my fate to please the gods and live forever.'

'Ah, but I slew Huwawa!' boasted Gilgamesh. 'And the Bull of Heaven! On my way here I slew a whole pride of lions!'

Utnapishtim looked unimpressed. 'May I suggest the gods might prefer their works of creation alive rather than dead?'

'Tell me,' said Gilgamesh tersely. 'Tell me how

you came to be immortal.' And all the while, Gilgamesh was thinking, 'What can this man do that I can't?'

So Utnapishtim told his story.

* * *

When Enlil began creating the world, his fellow gods did all the digging. But long before the last river bed was dug, the gods threw down their spades and pick-axes and refused to do another stroke.

Then the little god We-e came up with a solution. Why not create some kind of creature to complete the work? That is why human beings were created. They were ideal! When they could not work anymore, they died. But there were still enough, because they bred at such a rate! Soon cities grew up, swarming like ant hills with industrious little people.

The only snag was the noise they made. All day long they quarrelled and laughed, bartered goods in the markets, sang or made speeches.

They left their babies out in the sunshine and the mewling was more than Enlil could stand.

'What is that noise?' demanded Enlil.

'It's the people,' and Ea. 'Busy little things, aren't they?'

'Thin them out!' hissed Enlil. 'Send Plague to prune the noisiest.'

Ea had grown fond of humankind and hurried off to warn them. So when Plague arrived, the cities of Earth were silent as mirages, the citizens moving about with fingers on lips, the market traders miming, the babies' mouths plugged up with honeycomb. Plague turned round and went home.

While they stayed silent, Enlil was happy to let them live. But as time passed, of course, the noise built up again: nagging, squabbling and cheering.

'Silence their screeching!' yelled Enlil out of the windows of Heaven. 'Send Drought and Famine! Perhaps then these humans will finally be quiet!'

Again, Ea hurried off to warn the people of Earth. Once again the cities fell silent. Once again Enlil relented; Drought and Famine were packed away for another day.

But as time passed, of course, the noise built up again: wars and fairs, circuses and parades, building sites and forges.

Enlil slammed shut the windows of Heaven,

but it made no difference. 'DROWN THE WHOLE PACK OF THEM!' he bawled.

This time he summoned all his brother and sister gods and made them agree to the destruction of mankind. 'Not a warning word to a soul. Yes?'

Shamash bowed his head in consent.

Anu grunted and put his fingers in his ears.

Even Nurgal of the Underworld agreed.

And Ishtar, goddess of love.

Ea, too, said yes, though in his heart he was trying to think of some way to rescue the situation. There might just be time to deliver a single message ...

Seven generations ago, Shurrupak was my city. I was King there. I built many temples for the worship of Ea – such a gentle, agreeable fellow. We were good friends, Ea and I. Ea wanted to warn me, but because of his vow he couldn't speak to me directly, of course. So he whispered into the *fabric of my house*, do you see? He whispered into its reed walls.

'Reed house! Reed house! Listen and pray!
And let your walls be felled today
To build a mighty floating craft:
A huge, pitch-covered, roofed-in raft
As tall, as long, as wide – all square
That those who board her might then be spared
The doom of Heaven's reckoning:
A Flood which will drown everything.
For seven days he must not sleep
Or life will perish in the deep!'

That night, when the wind blew on my house, the reeds whispered to me as I slept, and I dreamed what I had to do: save the future, simple as that. In a week, I had a boat.

It had seven decks, each one divided into nine sections – to keep the various animals apart. I made the reeds watertight with a melted pitch, oil and asphalt. It was big – unimaginably big. It covered an acre of ground, and the hull was square – a cube, in fact. Not a good shape for a boat, but the gods aren't boat builders, are they?

I loaded aboard my family, my animals – took one male and one female of every species, so that afterwards – after the Flood – they could restock the Earth. Birds too. I mean, what would the Earth be without its animals and birds? In the evening, the rain began. It turned the ground to slurry.

So I went aboard myself, slithering and sliding, battened down the last hatch. It was dark – only the hiss of the rain. But that rain was nothing.

Water seemed to well up from the ground – from the abyss under the Earth; the goddess of the underworld smashed all her dams and let water come spouting up. The seven judges of Hell came roaming through the land holding firebrands – great rods of lightning that they wedged between Heaven and Earth. That storm smashed everything.

Soon the boat was riding floodwaters over cities and plains and forest. I had to stay at my tiller every moment, or we could have foundered

against a spire or snagged on the branches of some tree. I couldn't afford to sleep. I could see now, why Ea had forbidden me to sleep.

At dawn the Lord of the Storm summoned up a black cloud that smothered the whole world.

You could hear people calling out to one another. As the rain beat on them, they all began to turn back to clay – to the substance they were made from ... And how can you sleep while that happens? Even the gods were afraid. They climbed to the upstairs rooms of Heaven, but the floodwaters cornered them even there.

You could hear the goddess Ishtar howling, because she had gone along with Enlil's wishes.

'Didn't I help to give them life? Now look at them – floating in the ocean like fish food!' She wasn't alone. All the gods put their hands over their mouths and wept at what they had done.

For six days and nights the storm went on. I didn't close my eyes or sleep. Not for one moment. Even when every animal and every child and every star seemed to be asleep, I stayed awake, hand on the tiller, praying. When the rain finally stopped on the seventh day, I looked out from my ark and what did I see?

... Nothing. There was nothing to see.

Nothing in any direction; just water, flat as any rooftop. I don't mind telling you: I sat down and wept. I lay down and cried like a child. The whole of mankind turned back to clay. The whole of nature sunk under countless fathoms of water.

My head was stuffed with sleep. I was reeling with weariness. At first I didn't trust my eyes when I saw it – about fourteen leagues away: an island! I blinked and bleared at it. Yes! A bare mountain tip, sticking up out of the water! I won't say I steered for the island. We just drifted up against it and there we were wedged.

For seven days we sat wedged on that mountaintop, while the flotsam drifted by: dolls, dishes, gates, wheels, bottles ...

On the seventh day, I brought a dove up on deck and let her go.

She flew away ... but clearly there was
nowhere for her to perch because she came back.
The next day I loosed a swallow. She flew away
too, but the land was still drowned, because back
she came.

On the ninth day I loosed a raven. She circled
slowly, into the sunny sky, then flew off. She
didn't come back. That was when I knew it was
safe to open up every hatch and free the animals
from below decks.

They lumbered out past me – left behind
a smell I won't even try to describe. I watched
them straying farther and farther away from
the ark. The mountainside gradually surfaced,
steaming in the sunshine.

I was easy enough to see from Heaven, easy
to pick off, if Enlil glanced down. So I cooked
up the sweetest smelling sacrifice I could muster
– fourteen cauldrons of perfumed oil – and the
fumes went up and filled the whole dome of the
sky with the sweetest smell imaginable.

The gods were drawn to it, like flies to honey,

like sharks to blood; they couldn't keep away.
They came sighing and floating through the
rain-washed air, snuffing up the smoke. Last
of all came Ishtar – lovely Ishtar – wearing a
necklace of jewels that were every colour ever
given a name – red, amber, yellow, green, blue,
indigo and violet.

When she saw the Flood was over, she pulled
it off and threw it into the sky. 'I shall remember
these days! By the jewels of my throat, I shall
never forget!' That's what she said.

She had invented the rainbow, you see.

Enlil came along, of course. When he saw my
boat – oh – I thought he would smash it with a
single thunderbolt.

'WHAT?' he yelled. 'HAS ONE OF THEM
ESCAPED? WHO WARNED HIM?'

I cowered down under a corner of the ark,
head between my knees, hands over my ears ...

But then I heard Ea speaking up for me –
reasoning with Enlil.

'Where would we be without mortals to

dig and tend the Earth, to press the oil for our
sacrifices, to build temples to us? Why create
the Earth at all, if it is only to stand empty like
a house on a hill, doors banging in the wind.
I didn't tell the man Utnapishtim about the
coming of the Flood: he had the wisdom to
dream it. For seven days and seven nights he kept
awake, steering the ark safely through the waves.
Should such a man die?'

I had crawled out of hiding to listen. When
Enlil turned and saw me, it was too late to duck
out of sight again, so I stood up. He ordered me
and my wife to go aboard the ark. With trembling
knees, we went up the gangplank again and knelt
down on the uppermost deck. Up came Enlil,
closer and closer, reaching out his hands.

Then, just when I thought I would die of fear,
he touched our foreheads and said, 'Live forever,
man and woman of Shurrupak. Make your home
on Paradise Shore, beyond the River of Death.
And live forever, as we gods do!'

Chapter 9
The bread of sorrow

'Your eyelids are heavy, King of Uruk. How long since you slept?'

Gilgamesh gave a start. 'A day. Two days, perhaps ... If only the gods would test *me* like they tested you!'

Utnapishtim exchanged a smile with his wife. 'No need. I will set you a test. I don't pride myself on what I did – I had no choice, and the gods helped me. But could *you* stay awake seven days and seven nights, if lives depended on it?'

'Of course!' said Gilgamesh, jumping to his feet, eyes wide, despite their red rims.

What was so hard about defeating sleep, after all? Did it have claws or horns or fangs? Did it come wearing armour? No. Sleep was soft and wool-lined. Sleep came, swirling and silken, rolling over a man like fog.

The sea whispered behind Gilgamesh. The ropes of the hammock creaked in the tree.

Gilgamesh sat down again and rested his eyes for a moment. Weary? He had never been weary as a young man. How long ago was that? When had he paced about his palace too full of energy to sleep? Not so very long ago, surely? Was old age already flying towards him like a vampire bat, to drain him dry of energy? For a moment, he thought he saw it coming and opened his eyes in fright. But it was only the awning flapping, flapping in the sea-whispering breeze ...

'Wife,' said Utnapishtim, as Gilgamesh slumped sideways into sleep. 'Go and cook a loaf and set it down by our guest for him to eat when he wakes.'

'He won't wake for a week, poor weary soul,' said Saba.

'I know that,' said Utnapishtim. 'But bake it anyway.'

Every morning, Saba baked a loaf of bread and set it by Gilgamesh where he slept. They lay like seven pillows beside the sleeping King of Uruk.

When at last he stirred, his eyes struggled to focus. The next moment he was on his feet, swaying slightly with dizziness.

'That was a great sleep, Gilgamesh,' said Utnapishtim. 'A great sleep born of a great weariness.'

'Sleep? Me? No, no! I just nodded for a moment. Not asleep. I wasn't asleep!'

'For seven days and seven nights you slept, my friend.'

'Never! What do you take me for, a fool?'

'Each day I had my wife bake a loaf. Look. There they are. You can see how old they are. The first is green with mould, the last is still warm. In between are all the stages a loaf goes through before it ceases to be a loaf. A little like the life of man, wouldn't you say? Sweet smelling and softly tender at first. Harder with age. A harder outer crust to defend a man against life's knocks. Little by little more and more brittle. Then at last – decay. Which loaf of bread are you, I wonder?'

Gilgamesh's reply was to kick the oldest loaf out to sea. It exploded into dust around his foot.

He had failed the challenge. His weary body had let him down. He had failed, and failure was a very bitter bread indeed, to a man like Gilgamesh.

'Sit down. Breakfast, my friend,' said Utnapishtim. 'My wife bakes very good bread, and what more does a man need to be happy than a loaf of bread, a jug of milk and good company? Give up your quest.

'The gods never meant you to live forever, so why spoil the life they did give you? Is the rainbow any less beautiful because it's short-lived? Or because you can't grasp hold of it? Consider, man. Perhaps it is beautiful exactly because it is rare and fleeting.'

But Gilgamesh was not listening. His heart had turned to mould like that first-made loaf. All his dreams had exploded into dust. He knelt in the sand and wept, banging his forehead on the ground, tasting his own salt tears run in at the corners of his mouth like spray from the River of Death.

Meanwhile, Urshanabi had brought his ferry close in to the beach to see if he could glimpse Gilgamesh.

Utnapishtim the faraway was angry. 'Ferryman, you were wrong to bring this man here. Take him away, and take yourself off, too!

You broke your promise by bringing him here. You have lost the right to be my ferryman.'

Urshanabi meekly bowed his head in apology, accepting his banishment from Paradise Shore. He helped Gilgamesh aboard and put out to sea again. The mast was mended now; a new sail caught the warm wind. Gilgamesh sat huddled in the stern, still weeping.

'I feel so sorry for the man,' said Saba watching them go. 'He is so very, very afraid. My heart bleeds for him.'

Overhearing her words, Gilgamesh shuddered with shame.

'Am I a god? Could I have granted him immortality?' her husband asked in reply.

'You could have told him about Old-man-young. It's not immortality, but it would have been something. Something in return for his sufferings.'

Utnapishtim shook his head. 'Already he has exhausted his youth and strength on this foolish quest. It would be too great an ordeal ... too terrible ... *Ah*!'

'*Tell me what?*' Gilgamesh, hearing the conversation, had grabbed the helm, turned the boat about and run it ashore again.

Now he grabbed hold of Utnapishtim by the shoulders. '*What did she mean? Tell me!*'

'Old-man-young! Old-man-young!' cried Utnapishtim. 'Calmly, man! Put me down. It is the name of a plant.'

'*Is that where it grows? What does it look like? What does it do? How will I find it? Tell me!*'

So Utnapishtim told Gilgamesh about Old-man-young: a single weed growing off-shore, among dangerous, ripping currents. The plant was armed with thorns so sharp that even the crabs could not slice it with their armoured claws. 'Grip it tight, fetch it up to the light and eat it: it has magic enough to make a hundred old men young again,' said Utnapishtim. But whereas there had been friendship in his eyes before, there was a faraway look now. He was saddened by Gilgamesh's bad manners.

Chapter 10
The plant of life

'I shan't use it first myself,' Gilgamesh told the ferryman.

He sat tying rocks to his ankles with cords from the ferry's rigging. 'I'll give it to the old men of Uruk and see them grow young again. Imagine! The wisdom of old age in the body of a young man! Uruk will be the greatest city in all the world!'

The rocks scraped the skin from his ankle-bones, but he hardly noticed. They were to keep him from bobbing up to the surface too soon. He would have to hold his breath all the time. Filling his lungs to bursting point, Gilgamesh plunged into the sea.

The cold clamped his ribs and forced air out of him. The current turned him over and over; the rocks tied to his ankles struck his head and body and legs. He no longer knew which way up he was – which way to struggle for air.

He opened his clenched eyes and saw only swirling sand and bubbles. How far had he been swept? He peered ahead, hand clapped over nose and mouth, trying to keep the air in his chest. Gradually the water became clearer, but the tide rip shoved at him like a battering ram.

And there it was, on the seabed – a dark green snaggle of leaves and spiky stalks. No other plant grew in the strong current – only this one weed, too well rooted to be dislodged. Gilgamesh would have only one chance. If he failed to grasp the plant, he would be swept on by and lose it forever. He scuffed his feet, elbows, knees against the seabed to slow down, then grabbed the plant with both fists.

It was nettle and briar and cactus in one. The pain was so intense he thought the plant must be on fire, his hands burning. He opened his mouth to yell, and the sea rushed in.

But he did not let go.

He fumbled left-handed at the knots tying the rocks to his ankles; they were swollen and would

not undo. They would hold him down below water while he drowned. High above him, the sunny surface shimmered.

He picked up one of the rocks and sliced at the rope with it, all the while holding fast to the fabulous plant with its bristles and spines and spiky stalks.

His lungs flattened inside him. Blackness ringed his vision. If he let go, he might still live.

Then one foot was free, and the loop of the second was slipping over his heel. He set both feet on the seabed, pushed with all his might, and wrenched the plant out of the ocean floor.

He was not sure how he reached the surface. His whole head, his very lungs seemed to be full of seawater. And yet he burst through, brandishing the plant high above his head.

Choking and spluttering, he instantly began to kick his legs and drag the water aside with his left hand. But his right kept tight hold of the blazing agony, the precious weed.

His triumph felt wonderful. Not since Enkidu

fought at his side, not since the Bull of Heaven crashed to earth at his feet had Gilgamesh felt a joy like it. Like red hot needles, the plant's bristling spines pierced and cut his palm, but he could bear any amount of pain. The fear that had sat in his stomach ever since Enkidu's death was gone at last.

Not immortal, perhaps, but young again and full of vigour. He would have the time and strength to do such deeds that the gods would gape down and say, 'Look! Look at this Gilgamesh! Shall such a man die? Never!'

Gilgamesh trod water. He could not see the shore. He had used up all his strength in picking the plant.

What if the current was sweeping him out to sea? What if it washed him as far as the River of Death? What good would the plant be to him then?

Then he rolled over ... and, to his great joy, saw the fresh-painted prow of Urshanabi's ferry boat.

As Urshanabi pulled him aboard, Gilgamesh prattled and babbled. He whirled Urshanabi about in a wild, wet dance, and Urshanabi laughed and struggled, nodded and danced. He had grown fond of the crazy King of Uruk.

Suddenly Gilgamesh wanted very much to be home – to tell his mother, to see his shady rooms again, to know how the building work was getting on. He should not have left his people in a time of drought. Was that any way for the father of his people to behave? Suddenly he stopped dancing. 'Urshanabi! What have I done to you? I've put you out of work!' Urshanabi shrugged. 'Come home with me, Urshanabi. Come back to Uruk. There's no place in the world like Uruk.'

As the two men sailed back over the ocean, the seawater dried on Gilgamesh and left him salt-streaked. Brown blood caked his hands and arms, and his hair was seeded with saltwater prawns. He felt less like a king than a sardine drying in the sun.

They travelled back through the Garden of
the Gods, gathering up gemstones from under
the flower bushes. Unlike flower petals, though,
gemstones are heavy to carry, so they let them
fall again.

Gilgamesh spotted a lake and decided to
bathe. He set the plant down on a flat rock, and
sank himself in the cool water. His grey hair
spread out around his face as he floated on his
back, looking up at the sky. Soon he would be
wearing linen again and eating stoned olives and
taking a glass of cold, fresh milk on the sill of
his room in the Uruk palace. He would offer up
sacrifices, making things right with the gods.

He would ask their blessing on the people
of his city, then summon the masons to carve
his adventures on the bare wall. He would give
Urshanabi some post in government. 'Poor man!
To think I did that to him.'

He thought of Siduri, the cheery woman on
the seashore, and the face she had pulled when
he showed her the plant. 'Achh. You think this

bit of salad makes you happy? Take a wife! Have a child!'

The cool clean water crept in at his ears and the corners of his mouth and eyes. He was very happy. There were good people in the world – more than he had thought.

Glancing towards the rock, Gilgamesh saw
the green plant – a tatter of thorns and spines.
He saw the snake, too – of no great size: just
a common snake. It slithered out of a crevice,
tasting a peculiar scent on the air with its
quivering forked tongue.

'*NO!*'

It crossed the rock in a twinkling, unhinged its
jaws and swallowed down the plant, insensitive
to pain.

'*NO! NO! NO!*'

At once, its dull mantle of scales split from
end to end, and a new snake emerged, shining
and brightly coloured. Then it was gone, leaving
behind the transparent husk of its old skin,
leaving behind its old age.

Not a stem, not a leaf, not a bristle or a thorn
remained of the plant called Old-man-young.
All its magic – every twinkle and shimmer – was
gone too, down into the snake's belly.

Chapter 11
Home

Gilgamesh knelt on the bank of the pool gulping sobs. He beat his torn fists on the ground and howled like a wild animal.

'Gone, Urshanabi! What was it all for? All those weeks! All that suffering and pain! What am I? Nobody! Some old man with nothing to take home but tears!'

'Oh, I wouldn't say –' Urshanabi murmured comfort, but Gilgamesh was deaf to comfort.

They stumbled back through the Mountains of Mashu – somehow it was not so dark with two. Besides, the darkness inside Gilgamesh was ten times as black.

They travelled back through the Gates of Shamash, where the Scorpionguards stared at them in astonishment.

They travelled back through the mountain pass where the lions had prowled. There seemed to be just as many as before. But now Gilgamesh was startled by their beauty. Their hides suited them better than they had suited him. He did not want to slaughter them; they would be soon enough dead, poor beautiful beasts.

'Tell me about Uruk,' said Urshanabi, and Gilgamesh was eager to do so.

'The city is one part fields, one part town, one part gardens. Then there are the temples, of course – wonders of the world! The water from the river is carried by aquaducts through the city – threads of silver everywhere, like wire in a tapestry. The wall is high and curved. The foundations were laid in the days of the Seven Sages. Even when the Bull of Heaven stamped, the walls stayed standing!'

Urshanabi listened without interrupting.

'My builders are the best. My masons take pride in their work, and my gardeners are skilled at grafting and pruning...'

'I wonder you ever left such a place,' Urshanabi remarked mildly.

So too did Gilgamesh, when he saw Uruk.

Each familiar roof and tower and window was like the features of a well-loved face.

The perfumes of his childhood came to the gate to meet him. At least he had lived to see it all again.

As he walked through the streets, people idly looked up at the two grubby strangers. A murmur of excitement built up in their wake.

'Can it be?'

'It can't be!'

'The King, you mean? Never! He's long dead, surely!'

'Come and see! Go and tell the children!'

'Look! Look! Gilgamesh the mighty has come home!'

'Where are the banners?'

'See how white his hair ...'

'Where has he been?'

An inexpressible tenderness filled Gilgamesh. After being in lonely, distant places, it was good to see so many familiar faces. After the brown of the stony wilderness, the black of the mountain's

interior, he wondered at the colours of the city. He had forgotten how many flowers there were, how the awnings and drying washing added to the gold of masonry, the red of the terracotta. He had forgotten all the noises, too – women singing, dogs barking, chickens cackling, donkeys braying, the market traders shouting. Only the sound of building had fallen quiet, with no one to order new towers or temples.

A woman's voice drifted from a window.

'… worst news I've heard all year. I suppose now we must go back to war and hard labour?' She came to her window and looked out – straight into the face of the King. Her eyes, already fearful, widened into terror as she realised he had heard her. She was afraid for her life.

Gilgamesh offered her a smile – an awkward, grimacing smile, realising he was not very good at smiling. He would have to practise.

At his shoulder, the ferryman stood gazing about him.

'Well, Urshanabi? Didn't I say it was the finest

city in the world?'

Urshanabi smiled and nodded. At last Gilgamesh's tour of the city brought them to the carved friezes depicting the deeds of past heroes. There was Utnapishtim, his odd square ark wedged on a mountaintop.

There were the Seven Sages ... and there were Enkidu and Gilgamesh bringing home the tallest tree from the Cedar Forest to build new gates for Uruk.

'And this, I take it, is Enkidu,' said the ferryman.

Gilgamesh had left Uruk before the scene was carved. At first he could not bear to look. Then he looked and could not stop looking. His hand reached out towards the figure carved high up, far larger than life. His fingers came to rest on the ankle of Enkidu. 'I came back, friend. Just as I was, but I came back.' Urshanabi saw that his eyes were full of tears.

The ferryman smiled and shook his head. Nothing could be farther from the truth.

Chapter 12
The twelfth tablet

The skies over Uruk were smoky as the King's sacrifices burned – meat and fruit, oil and flowers. The gods were drawn like flies to circle in the perfumed air. After fulfilling his duty to the gods, Gilgamesh sent for his masons. The people groaned: now the building would begin again; soon it would be the wars.

But Gilgamesh was too weary for battle campaigns. Since destroying the steering gear of the ferryboat, he thought twice about destroying things. Fearing Death, he no longer wished it on the young men of his army.

Exhausted, he no longer wanted anyone to work themselves into an early grave. He did not want anyone to mourn, as he had mourned for

Enkidu. He looked at the old men and felt responsible for them.

He sent for his masons and scribes. He told them to carve his adventures on the wall of heroes and to write them on clay tablets for future generations to read.

While he told them his story, they listened like children at his feet, open-mouthed, fingers in their hair, astounded. They ran home and told their families, and soon the city buzzed with voices retelling the epic of Gilgamesh. What a story it was!

The King relived his adventures in his dreams. Sometimes he woke crying, sometimes screaming. Sometimes he even woke up laughing.

Through his window he heard the people say, 'He has changed! How he has changed!'

But how could that be? He had not gained immortality. He had not eaten the prickly plant. Surely it was *they* who had changed. Once they had hated him, and now, for some reason, they

seemed to love him.

When the frieze was finished, he went to look at it. 'But tell me – why this empty panel at the end? Do you think I will be going on more journeys?' asked Gilgamesh wryly.

'No, sire. But begging your pardon, sire, that panel is to show your funeral ...'

Gilgamesh rocked on his heels. He went back to the palace and asked to see what his poets had written about him. They brought him eleven tablets.

'I suppose you realise this is incomplete?' he said, harsh and rasping. 'You have not recounted my death.'

The poets bowed low. 'Naturally, there will be twelve tablets, lord King.'

* * *

At last, Gilgamesh took to heart the advice of Siduri, the woman with the cats on the seashore. He did marry. One year later, his first son was born. He took the child in his arms and stood on the broad sill of his room overlooking the city. Tears ran down his cheeks as freely as the day his friend had died.

But today he was crying for joy.

For wasn't he holding New Life in his arms? And didn't it have his eyes and his hands and his long feet and his Sumerian nose? Was he not immortal now? As immortal as every other father whose children and children's children will live on after him? The child's hand within his own was as small as the seed of a cedar tree. It would grow.

He named his son Prince Enkidu.

* * *

Out of the darkness, a dream hurtled down – a meteor trailing a tail of light, an axe lying at Gilgamesh's feet. The meteor was fame, the axe his fate. They were heavy to carry, but no one else would have even tried to pick them up. As it was, Gilgamesh did such things, dared so much, learned such wisdom, conquered such fear that his name outlived the gods themselves.

Long after Enlil and Anu, Ishtar, Ea and Shamash had been forgotten on the Plain-of-Two-Rivers, the fame of Gilgamesh lived on. He was Gilgamesh the mortal, Gilgamesh the friend, Gilgamesh the father, Gilgamesh the hero, Gilgamesh the coward, Gilgamesh the wise man, Gilgamesh the fool. Everyone wants to leave their mark on the world, and he left a mark as big as a meteor crashing to Earth.

He walked through darkness and so glimpsed the light.